Written by Anne Schreiber

Illustrated by Debbie Pinkney

SCHOLASTIC INC.

New York Toronto London Auckland Sydney

For my brother, Barry

-A.S.

Printed in the U.S.A.
ISBN 0-590-27389-2

7 8 9 10 09 00 99 98 97 96

This oak tree has been living in the forest for a hundred years.

One day, a strong wind
knocks the tree down.
The tree falls to the ground.
Now the tree is a log.

Soon ants and beetles move in and eat the log. They drill small tunnels in the log as they eat. The tunnels help to make the log soft as it decays.

This woodpecker is listening
for bugs inside the log.
As soon as it hears a bug,
it drills through the bark
to catch it. Tap, tap, tap. . . .

Soon living things called
fungi grow on the log.
Inside the log, fungi
look like spaghetti.
Outside the log, fungi
look like mushrooms.

Snails and slugs move in. They creep through the tunnels as they hunt for fresh fungi and dead beetles and ants to eat. The tunnels get bigger. The log gets softer.

A snake slithers through the log. It is looking for a place to rest for the winter.

Soft moss grows on the log.
Green ferns grow in and
around the log.

This log is like a plant and animal hotel. As time goes on, more and more plants and animals move in.

The log gets softer and softer.
Now the shape of the log
is hard to see. Earthworms eat
what is left of the log.

The earthworms turn what
they eat into soil. The soil
is the perfect place
for a seed to grow.

The seed will grow into a tree.
One day, the tree will fall.
It, too, will become
a log hotel.